# OVERDOSES IN OLYMPIA

## CAPITAL CITY MURDERS #1

TROY LAMBERT

STUART GUSTAFSON

Published by
CCMbooks
P.O. Box 45091
Boise, ID 83711 USA
www.capitalcitymurders.com

First Printing June 2019
This is a work of fiction. Names, characters, businesses, places, events and
incidents are either the products of the authors' imaginations or used in a
fictitious manner. Any resemblance to actual persons, living or dead, or
actual events is purely coincidental

 Created with Vellum

In the meantime, be well. Nick and I will see you as we travel the country together!

# PROLOGUE

Prologue — Another Overdose

Mary slipped her arms into the white sweater, the one with the name tag Mary Lawson, RN attached. She took one final sip of her coffee, poured out the rest, and paused. *What did I miss? The patient had come in with a shattered right leg and an arm broken in two places. Thank God he was wearing a helmet, or he might have been taken to the morgue instead of to the hospital. He seemed healthy other than the injuries from the motorcycle accident.*

She'd been racking her brain for the past two days trying to figure out what happened, why the accident victim overdosed. He was under her care, and she did everything that any nurse would do in the same situation. The odd part was, the patient had been almost ready to go home.

Sure, he seemed a bit melancholy, but who wouldn't be after that kind of accident? It seemed odd.

There would be an autopsy, of course, and that would show exactly what caused his death. That would take at least two weeks.

Mary looked at her watch. She should be heading to work. The drive to Mercy Hospital took her past the location on the freeway where the motorcycle had been sideswiped, and she grimaced as she passed the spot. There was a piece of shiny metal on the right shoulder she hadn't seen before. Was it from the accident?

"Good morning, Mary," the guard said as Mary pulled into the employees' secure parking area and lowered her window.

"Good morning, John," she replied. "How's it going?"

"Pretty quiet so far," he answered as he pushed the button to raise the gate. "Have a good day."

"You, too." Mary raised her window and drove to her favorite parking spot. Close to an entrance, it was shaded in the afternoon. She disliked getting into a hot car, but even worse she hated leaving the windows down and having the elm leaves blow inside. There was something in those leaves that set off her allergies and made her sneeze uncontrollably.

Once inside, Mary put her purse in her locker and took the staff elevator to the fourth floor.

"Good morning, Pat," Mary said as she approached the nurses' area.

Pat looked up from her paperwork. "Hi, Mary. You know I am always glad to see you, and not just because you're taking over."

"I know. I see a new name on the board. What's he in for?"

"Mainly observation," the departing nurse said. "He works at a lumber mill and was hit in the head with more than just the proverbial two by four. A CT scan didn't show any abnormalities, but the ER doc wanted to hold him for twenty-four hours just to make sure. He will probably go home sometime during your shift, so you'll give him his instructions and meds to go home with."

"Well, let's go over the shift handoff report so you can go home and get some rest," Mary said as she pulled a chair.

Mary started her own rounds thirty minutes later. She entered room 414, the one with the new patient. The woman who'd been in there for the last few days had gone home last night. The room was now Robert's, and his alone at least for the next few hours. A putrid smell hit her as she stepped further inside.

*Flatulence. The kitchen needs to stop serving so much beans and broccoli.*

She cleared her throat as she stepped around the curtain to see her new patient, who completely filled the length of the standard hospital bed.

Robert looked up at her and smiled.

"Good morning, Robert. My name is Mary Lawson, and I'm the RN on duty, so you'll be seeing a lot of me today." She caught his eyes checking her out. Her face flushed slightly as she tried to maintain her composure.

She cleared her throat.

"How are you feeling? I see in your chart that you took quite a blow to the head." Mary glanced up from the screen that held his electronic patient chart.

Robert extended his right hand over his reclining body as Mary awkwardly reached across the space separating them and shook his hand. He could probably fit both her hands inside one of his. "Nice to meet you, Mrs. Lawson," he said in a deep voice.

"It's Miss Lawson, but that's okay. Actually, Mary is fine."

What was this awkward feeling coming over her?

Mary gently pulled her hand back. "Your hand seems a

bit cool," she said as she looked at his vitals that had been taken just about an hour ago. "Are you in any pain right now?"

"I do have a headache, but the doc last night said I probably would for a few days. It's pretty normal considering. He also said I might be able to go home today?"

"That's up to him," Mary said and looked back at the chart. "You've had enough acetaminophen that it should've taken care of your pain, but I can get you something stronger if you'd like."

"Sure," he said. "That would be great. If the doc could send me home with something just in case, that would be good too."

"I'll get some prescription naproxen for you. Like Aleve, only a little stronger. Have you had that before?"

Robert shrugged. "I think so."

"Okay. I'll bring some in a bit and see if I can get you a bottle to go, so to speak. Need anything else at the moment?"

He just smiled and looked up at her through his arched bushy eyebrows. "No, ma'am. Thank you."

Mary felt warm. She unconsciously grabbed the front of her sweater and flapped it to try to cool herself down. "You're welcome, Robert, but you don't have to thank me. That's what we're here for, to help you get better. I should be back within a few moments with something for that pain." Mary turned and left the room. She sensed Robert's eyes following her until the curtain blocked his view.

A few minutes later, Mary made it back into room 414, carrying a small dispensing cup holding two capsules. "Knock, knock," she said as she entered the room. Some sports station was on the television. The same odor hit her as she stepped past the curtain. "Who's winning?"

"They are just replaying old games," Robert said as he used his bulging arms to push his body into a more upright position.

"Thank you," Robert said as he tossed the capsules to the back of his mouth and swallowed them without any water.

"If you drink something, it will help them get into your system faster."

"Yes, ma'am," he replied as he took the cup of water from the tray and emptied it in three huge gulps.

"I'll be back later to check on you. Maybe even to send you home. Need anything else?"

"No, ma'am," Robert said as he let his long, well-muscled body slide back down into the bed. Her eyes instinctively watched his movements as if in slow motion.

"I'll close the door, but you can always press your call button if you need anything." Mary pulled the door closed behind her. The cool air in the hall felt really good.

A few hours passed quickly, and around the time for her noon rounds, Mary got the discharge papers for room 414. She gathered up the prescription bottle of capsules the pharmacy had sent up. Pulling up the forms for him to sign on her tablet, she made her way to his room.

Since her hands were full, she knocked softly and went in. The room was now very quiet, and the odor that previously plagued the room was gone.

Robert was laying on his side, sleeping, and she woke him gently.

"Robert?"

He sat up, still seeming to be a bit groggy. Not a great sign for a guy who might have had a concussion. "I'm awake," he managed to say.

"Let me check a few things really quick," Mary said, a bit concerned.

She took out her penlight and shined it in each eye. Pupils were reactive. She felt the pulse on his neck, and it felt strong and normal.

"You seem to be okay. I'm going to have you sign these discharge papers. We do it on these tablets now, and then I can print it out for you. But I am going to have the doctor check you out before you leave."

Robert smiled, seeming to be coming back from his impromptu nap. "Sounds good. I guess those pills really did help with the headache."

"Here are your ones to take home," she told him. "No more than one every twelve hours. You can get dressed now, and I will be right back."

Mary walked down the hall to the nurses' station, hitting the print button as she went.

She grabbed Robert's paperwork as it spat out of the printer. Reaching for the phone to page the doctor on call, she saw the call light came on above his door and heard the chime at the desk.

Without hesitating, Mary sprinted down the hall back to the room. She heard a crash as she opened the door.

Robert was on the floor, face red as if he was choking. Lying beside him on the floor was an open pill bottle.

For a moment, she caught a whiff of almonds.

Mary knelt beside him and felt his neck for a pulse. There wasn't one.

She dropped his arm and pressed the call button again, yelling into the speaker: "Crash cart! Stat. Four fourteen. Now!"

Immediately she started CPR. Help seemed to take an eternity to arrive, even though she knew it was only seconds. Her arms already felt heavy as she continued compressions on his chest.

A doctor arrived followed closely by another nurse pushing a cart. Mary moved aside as the doctor put his stethoscope to the man's hairy chest.

"Still no pulse," he said.

The other nurse turned on the fully charged defibrillator. "Ready," she said.

The doc grabbed the paddles and placed them on the patient's chest. "Clear," he said, and the nurse flipped the switch. Mary watched in haunted silence as Robert's body shook from the electric charge coursing through him. The doctor listened again for a heartbeat. There was none. He applied the paddles again. Another shock. Still nothing.

He threw the paddles aside and resumed CPR, pressing down hard on the chest and counting aloud, "One, two, three." Doc counted to ten and placed his ear near the patient's mouth. Still no breath. After several futile attempts, he stood back.

"He's gone, I'm sorry." The doc looked at the bottle and capsules on the table. "He must've overdosed."

"Why would he do that?" Mary said. "He was on his way out."

"I have no idea," the doctor said.

*No!* Mary's mind churned in anguish. *Not another overdose! And both of them had occurred when she was on duty.*

1
_______

## THE DRIVE

Nick looked at the map he'd downloaded for the short drive from Seattle to Olympia. *Straight down I-5; that's simple enough.* He looked at his cell phone to see if there were any new messages. None.

He selected the phone icon, then the Recent Calls menu. He saw the number he wanted, and he pressed it. The phone on the other end rang. It rang four more times before it went to voicemail and the ensuing beep. *Rats.* "Hello, Mr. Lam. This is Nick O'Flannigan calling on Sunday afternoon about two thirty. I was hoping to have an answer from you about sub-letting my apartment while I'm out of town. Please give me a call. My number is 7 8 1 ... 5 5 5 ... 8 4 2 3. Thank you." He ended the call and returned the phone to his pocket.

Nick looked around the front room of his apartment. He picked up the folder he'd labeled "The Assignment," opened it, and started reading the top sheet, a short one-page letter. He'd read it many times before, and a smile came across his face as he began reading it again.

Dear Nick,

Per our recent phone conversation, we at *Travel USA* magazine are delighted to offer you a one-year contract to provide us with unique and interesting photographs of each U.S. state capitol building and surrounding areas. You were selected for this prestigious assignment because of your excellent photographic background and skills, your keen attention to detail, and a very strong recommendation from one of our most valued employees, Gerry Grainger. Attached is the sequence that you are to follow for visiting each state capital. Please do not deviate from that schedule.

As a reminder, time is essential, and you are expected to spend no more than one week in each city, while traveling on weekends. You are to submit your photographs no later than Saturday for that week's capital city, and email that week's expense report, including lodging, gas, and per diem allowance no later than Sunday. Your timely submissions will enable us to prepare and remit the electronic payment to your bank account within five days.

Should you have any questions, now or while you're on the road, do not hesitate to contact me.

Respectfully yours,


THE LETTER WAS SIGNED Emily Gorham, Executive Editor, *Travel USA* magazine.

He looked at his checklist; he'd checked everything off. It took several elevator trips for Nick to get everything loaded into his car. He made one last pass through the apartment, switched off all the lights, and locked the door as he left.

*Goodbye, apartment. See you in a year.*

Nick had picked a good time for the drive south to Olympia. Traffic was very light through Seattle. His hands-free phone in the dashboard cradle rang. "Hello," he said as he pressed the flashing icon.

"Hello, Nicholas. This is your mother calling." She was only one besides his father who called him by his given name.

"Hi, Mom. How's everything in Boston?"

"We're fine. We were just ready to sit down for supper, and your father suggested we call and see how your new job is going."

"It's just starting today, and it's not actually a job. I'm on a contract assignment for the magazine, and I'm in the car right now driving down to Olympia, Washington's state capital."

"It's not a job, Patrick," she yelled away from the phone to Nick's dad who was in another room. "He says it's a contract."

"The difference, Mom, is that I'm not an employee of the magazine. They're just paying me to take photographs for them. It's kind of like what Dad did when he got out of the Navy. Remember when he worked for that electronics firm? He was a contractor for them, not an employee who got benefits from them besides a paycheck."

"I don't really understand it, but that's okay," she said. "So, how long are you going to be gone?"

"I told you before, Mom. I'll be gone for a year. I'll spend a week at most in each capital city, and it'll be about ten to eleven months before I'm there in Boston. They have a set schedule for me to follow. It's actually a pretty good route even though the cities are farther apart here on the west coast than they are out East."

"If you're gone for a year, what's going to happen to your business you worked so hard to re-establish after you left here? Isn't that a waste to just throw all that away?"

Nick exhaled deeply. He hesitated slightly before answering. "No, Mom, I'm not throwing it all away. I do most my business online, and I can do that from anywhere."

"What about your apartment? Who's going to take care of it?"

He spoke slower. "I'm hoping to be able to sub-let it while I'm gone. But even if I can't, I have enough savings to cover it. I'll be fine, Mom. I'm not a little kid anymore."

"I know, big shot. You're a six-foot-six former college basketball star, but that doesn't mean your Mother still doesn't worry about you."

"I know, Mom. I didn't mean it that way. I'm sorry." He paused. "There's some traffic up ahead. I'd better go focus on the road. I love you, Mom. Tell Dad I love him too."

"I love you, too, Nicholas. Drive carefully."

"I will, Mom. Bye," he said as he disconnected the call.

*She'll never understand.*

Nick's bushy orange hair almost touched the roof of his car. His height had a few disadvantages, but a definite advantage when driving into the sun. He glanced down at the odometer and saw that he'd already driven twenty-six miles.

*Almost half-way there. It'd be nice if all the weekend travels were this short.*

On long drives, Nick usually listened to audio books, but in this case with such a short drive, he listened to podcasts. He especially liked this one, a couple of ex-policemen talking about murders they had seen and solved, and how. He was fascinated by how they made connections between things that seemed random but were not.

He had selected a hotel in Olympia that was not only a short distance off the freeway but was also within walking distance of the capitol. The nightly rate was within his lodging budget, and there was no parking fee.

The podcast ended, and Nick clicked off cruise control as he neared Olympia. There was some traffic congestion, and he wasn't familiar with the area, so he cut off the next episode so he could concentrate.

His map showed the freeway would make a sweeping curve to the right, and his exit would be before the turn back to the left. He watched the exit signs; his was next, Exit 105A.

Slowing as he left the freeway, Nick continued on Plum Street Southeast. A half mile farther, he took a left on Union Avenue Southeast. He'd seen on Google Maps that all the road names in this area were suffixed with "SE." Four blocks later he made a right turn on Franklin, and he saw his hotel up on the left at the next corner. The Capital City Inn was located on the northeast corner of Franklin Street and Tenth Avenue, both suffixed Southeast, of course.

Nick slipped his backpack on and grabbed two large rolling bags from the trunk. One bag contained clothing and the other bag was full of camera gear. As he walked into the office, the clerk glanced up from her work. Then she looked up even more, titling her head back to be able to look Nick in the face. "Welcome to the Capital City Inn, sir. Checking in?"

"Yes, I am. The last name is O'Flannigan."

"Certainly, Mr. O'Flannigan." The keys on her keyboard clicked for a short minute. "We have you here for six nights in a King room. Do you prefer ground floor or higher up?"

"Higher up would be nice, and one that faces south if possible. I'm here to take photographs of the capitol, and I think I just might be able to see down the North Diagonal to it, if I'm lucky."

"Let's see," the clerk said. "Ah, yes. Room 306 should be perfect. How many keys, Mr. O'Flannigan?" she asked as she once again leaned her head back to look at Nick.

"Just one, please. And do call me Nick. It's much easier."

"Certainly, Nick," she said as she put the key packet on the counter along with the pre-completed registration form. "If you'll just sign right there. Also add your car make and model and the plate number, here ... here ... and here. Still the same Visa card?"

Nick completed the form and set the pen down. "Yes, same card. Breakfast?"

"In the room right behind you from six until nine thirty. Someone's here twenty-four hours a day, so just dial zero if you need anything. Oh, the elevator's down the hall on your left."

"Thank you, Cindy," Nick said as he bent his head down to see her name tag.

"You're welcome, Nick. Hope you have a good stay."

"Thanks, I'm sure I will," Nick answered as he pulled his bags toward the elevator.

2
___________

MORNING PAPER

The early morning crowd was gone, and the late group was meandering in and out of the breakfast room as Nick entered. He wasn't in a rush to get going this morning. He would focus on special effect photos of the Capitol Building later in the week. Today was a day to take the "standard pictures" and get acquainted with the area. Even though he'd lived in Seattle for a few years and driven down I-5 to historic Astoria on the Oregon side of the Columbia River, Nick hadn't spent any time in Olympia. He had five more days here, plenty of time to check out the city of fifty-some-thousand.

Newspaper folded and tucked under his left arm, Nick headed first to the coffee station. *Hmm. Sabor Bravo Coffee. Wonder what they had to do to keep Starbucks out of this place?* He poured himself a full cup of steaming Dark Roast and took it to an empty table next to the window. He sat the cup down, then the paper, still folded in half, and made his way around the small buffet area to survey what was available.

Returning to the table with a plate of scrambled eggs, sausage, along with a banana and a yogurt cup, Nick sat down and took a sip of the hot coffee. *Good.* He took a bite of the scrambled eggs as he unfolded the newspaper with his left hand. He'd picked *The Capital Daily* instead of *USA Today* because he was interested in local news. His phone fed him national and international news on a regular basis. "Another Mercy Hospital Overdose" blared the headline along with a recent photo of the young victim accompanying the lead article. Nick read the article as he ate. *What luck. One poor guy's in a motorcycle accident and goes to the hospital with some broken bones. Then he over-doses the next day as he is being discharged. But then there's a second similar overdose at that hospital in just a week, both men about to leave. What's with the young people these days? They're both about my age. What could possibly drive them to overdose? What a waste.*

Nick went back for another plate of eggs and sausage, plus a glass of orange juice this time. It took a lot of energy to fuel his six-six frame. He skimmed through the paper, noticing an article about the Governor's reception for the media on Thursday evening. *I wonder if I can get invited to that.* He took out his pocket notebook and wrote a note: "Gov's office; get invite to Thurs. reception." The Sports section was mostly the local teams and leagues along with a few final scores from around the country. He grabbed the paper, put it back under his left arm and cleared the table.

There were a couple and a businessman checking out as he passed by the front desk on the way to the elevator. He got to his room, brushed his teeth, got his camera bag, and put the front section of the newspaper into the side pouch. He took the stairs down the lobby level and saw there was a new person at the front desk.

"Good morning," Nick said to the young man. "I'm in 306 for the week, and I don't know the area. Any suggestions close by for a really tasty lunch?"

The clerk's eyes scanned higher and his jaw opened wider at the sight of this "big man" standing there. "It all depends on what you like. Mexican, Italian, steak and potatoes, Chinese, Japanese, we have all kinds of restaurants close by," he said as he reached for a tourist map of downtown. "They're all listed on here."

The clerk took his pen and drew several continuous circles around the one at the northeast corner of Cherry and Twelfth. "This one's my favorite; it's a small Vietnamese place that has the best spring rolls. Plus, their lemon chicken is totally awesome."

"Thanks," Nick said as he smiled, took the map, and slid it into his bag next to the newspaper. "Have a great day." Nick turned, and strode out of the lobby, camera bag looped over his left shoulder. Once outside, he headed south on Franklin.

Centennial Park was on the opposite side of Union Street, the next block down. *Some interesting possibilities for photos,* he thought as he looked at the block-wide park. Ten minutes and two turns later, Nick was heading southwest on the North Diagonal leading to the Winged Victory statue. He stopped short, brought his camera out of the bag, and took a few shots with the Capitol Building in the background. He slung the camera around his neck.

*Not exactly like the one in the Louvre,* Nick thought as he got closer, *but it's still a nice representation.*

Taking pictures as he walked along, Nick's head brushed the bottom of a pine branch overhanging the sidewalk. He reached up with his left hand to rub the top of his bushy mane, much to the delight of a group of school children playing in the grass. Nick heard their giggles, so he turned, waved, and flashed a big smile at them. He snapped a few photos as they waved back at him.

Standing halfway between the Temple of Justice and the Legislative Building, aka, the Capitol Building, Nick couldn't get the proper focus on the capitol. *The sun is too high in the sky for this southerly shot,* he thought to himself. *The front's more important, anyway.* He put the camera away, walked around to the South Entrance, and went inside. "Where's the Governor's office?" he asked the security guard.

"He's out of town for the next couple of days," the guard volunteered.

"That's okay; it's his secretary I wanted to talk to," Nick responded as he retrieved his camera bag from the screening belt.

The guard, six feet tall himself, looked up at Nick. "Second floor, all the way down on your right," he said.

"Thanks," Nick said as he headed to the wide marble staircase and took the steps two at a time.

"Show off," Nick heard the guard mumble, and he grinned to himself.

"Back at 10:30," announced the printed sheet taped on the glass door leading to The Office of the Governor.

Nick looked at his watch, 10:20. He sat on the tufted velvet bench and pulled out the newspaper. He scanned the lead article again and looked at the photograph of the latest overdose victim. Nick's eyebrows furrowed as he squinted to focus on a small area of the picture. On the young man's neck, just below his left ear was a small tattoo. *I didn't see that earlier, but it looks like one I've seen online before. Too bad it's not a sharper photo.* Nick read the article again, folded the paper, and put it back in his camera bag. He looked at his watch, 10:38. *Oh, well. I'll check back with her.*

He grabbed his camera bag, slung it over the left shoulder, and headed back to the hotel.

## 3

## THE TATTOO

Nick walked into his room and saw that it was the same as when he'd left it not long ago. *That's okay. I don't really need anything,* he thought. He took the "Do Not Disturb" sign, slipped it around the door's front handle, closed it, and flipped the dead bolt. He picked up the desk phone and pressed the "Front Desk" button.

"Front Desk. How may I help you?"

"Yes, I'm in 306, and I plan to be working in my room today, so I put the 'Do Not Disturb' sign out. Will you please tell Housekeeping that I don't need anything today?"

"Of course, Mr. O'Flannigan. Is there anything else I can help you with?"

"No, thanks."

"Have a good day, sir."

"You, too," Nick said as he put the phone back down. He pulled the laptop out of his backpack, set it on the desk, opened it, and pressed the power button. As it was powering up, Nick went to the window and looked southwest toward the Capitol Building. He saw the North Diagonal he'd walked down, and the impressive—though not the same—Winged Victory statue.

He pulled the paper from the camera bag, sat down, opened the browser, and entered "tattoo images" in the Search field. Almost a billion results popped up. *Okay, let's try again.* He opened the paper and looked at the grainy photograph again.

Back to the browser. He typed in "thecapitoldaily.com" and hit the Enter key. There it was, front and center—the same photograph in the print newspaper, but a much sharper digital image. Nick right-clicked on the photo and selected "Save Image As..." opened the file, zoomed in on the tattoo, and immediately recognized it. There had been several postings on his "MacroPhotography4U.com" website of that same tattoo.

Nick went back to the newspaper's webpage. He clicked on the contact us tab, found their phone number and called it.

"The Capital Daily, how may I direct your call?"

"Local News Editor, please," Nick answered.

"Hold on, please."

"Local News Desk, how may I help you?"

"Hi. I'm a photographer who's here in town on a completely different assignment, but I think I might have something for your overdoses story."

"May I ask your name, please?"

"Sure. I'm Nick O'Flannigan. I'm from Seattle, but I'm on assignment from a major magazine to visit each U.S. state capital. That's why I'm here in Olympia."

"How do you spell that last name, sir?"

"Capital-O-apostrophe-Capital F-l-a-n-n-i-g-a-n."

"Thank you, sir. And what is it that you have?" the beleaguered voice continued.

"As I said, I'm a photographer, and I host a macro photography website that's focused on the small details in photographs." Nick continued. "I noticed the photograph in the paper this morning of the overdose victim, and he had a small tattoo on the left side of his neck. It's one I've seen several times before."

"Oh?" The voice sounded more interested.

"Unfortunately, it's a tattoo that represents a cult that likens itself to the Jonestown group. They often commit group or individual suicides as part of a strange pact using nightshades and other poisons. You know who they are, right?"

"Of course. So, what's the connection?"

"Your story said this was the second overdose victim at that hospital. Do you have any photographs of the first overdose victim? Did he have any tattoos, perhaps one like this?"

"Mister, uh, O'Flannigan, we can look into that. Is there a way we can reach you?"

"There is," Nick answered in a frustrated voice. "But we're talking about overdoses here. What is your paper going to say the next time a young person is admitted to the hospital and overdoses? What if the connection between the two victims is some kind of suicide pact?"

"Hold a minute while I get the editor on the phone."

"Thank you," Nick replied. *That's who I was trying to reach in the first place.* He glanced out the third-floor window; sitting tall in the chair he could see the very tip of Capitol Lake at the end of the Puget Sound.

"Hello," the new voice finally came on. "My name is Mark, the Local News Editor. You think the overdoses have something to do with a Jonestown copycat group?"

"I'm not saying that for sure, Mark. What I'm saying is that the tattoo on the young man in today's front page article is from a cult that is known to engage in suicide pacts. My question to you is if you have a photograph of the first overdose victim, does he have a similar tattoo?"

"Just a minute, please."

Nick got out of the chair and walked over to the window. The lake was in view, although it wasn't the best angle to see much of it. The view down the North Diagonal, past Winged Victory, to the Capitol was nice though. Cindy had given him a good room. *I need to get something for her.*

"Sorry for taking so long," the news editor said as he came back on. "We do have photos of the first victim, and he had no tattoos at all. They're still waiting for the autopsy report. But Mr. O'Flannigan, is it?"

"Yes?" Nick said.

"I can't share details with you anyway, of an ongoing police investigation or anything we are doing here at the paper. I do appreciate the call, and your concern though."

Nick thanked the editor, and hung up, disappointed. He really thought he'd been on to something for a minute there.

*You're not a detective, and you do have work to do,* he told himself as he put his phone down. *The editor told you as much just now.*

Maybe he should go get some lunch, come back and start fresh when his stomach wasn't growling so loudly.

4

—————————

## THE APARTMENT

Nick left the "Do Not Disturb" sign on his door as he left for lunch. He didn't grab his camera, just a notebook, pen, and his cell phone. He headed for that small Vietnamese restaurant about six blocks away. His cell phone vibrated and then played the opening bars of "For Boston." Even though he'd been away for a few years and hadn't been back to alma mater Boston College since his graduation, he liked hearing the B.C. fight song.

"Hello, this is Nick." He squinted his eyes, not recognizing the voice at first. Then the caller identified himself.

"Oh, yes, Mr. Lam. Thank you for calling. Of course, I will still be responsible for paying the rent and covering any damages if there's a problem. The rent is on auto-pay, so it'll be in your account the first of every month just like it's been for the past year."

Nick stopped under the shade of a large oak as he listened to his landlord.

"Thank you, Mr. Lam. I know the lease said no sub-letting, and I really appreciate your making this accommodation for me. There is a renter who was very interested. I'll send you his contact information just as soon as I finalize the details with him. That is, unless he's found a different place by now."

"Yes, sir." Pause. "Yes, Mr. Lam. Thank you again." Pause. "You, too. Good bye for now," Nick said as he ended the call. *I hope Ben is still interested,* he thought.

He reached the restaurant a few moments later and went in to eat.

"YES, I'll have the spring rolls and the lemon chicken, please," Nick said as the waiter approached. "And a large iced tea," he added. Nick pulled out his phone and checked his email messages. He put away his phone, took a sip of water, and then he heard a loud crash behind him. He turned around and saw a young man on his knees hurriedly picking up the broken dishes and bowls that had just fallen from his tray.

"Sorry about that noise," Nick's waiter said as he delivered a small plate of spring rolls, a large plate of white rice topped with lemon chicken, and the glass of iced tea. "Anything else for now?"

Nick looked over the two plates, and then to the waiter. "No, thanks."

Nick cut into one of the spring rolls and a line of steam rose toward the ceiling. He picked up a piece with chopsticks, dipped it into the sauce, and ate it. He smiled as he enjoyed the flavor combination of the vegetables and the tangy sauce. He leaned over slightly to catch the aroma of the thick lemon sauce on the chicken. *Hmmm.* He worked his chopsticks on the chicken and the rice, occasionally alternating with part of a spring roll until both plates were fairly empty. A few pieces of rice were left on the large plate, but that was all.

"Excellent," Nick said as the waiter came by and left the tray with the bill and a wrapped fortune cookie. He took the wrapper off the fortune cookie, cracked it open, and chuckled as he read his "fortune." He got up, paid the bill, left the restaurant and headed back to the hotel. He stopped in Centennial Park and sat on a bench in the shade. He pulled out his phone. "Call Ben," he commanded the phone.

"Calling Ben," the phone responded as he put it up to his ear.

"This is Ben."

"Hey Ben, it's Nick O'Flannigan. I just got off the phone with my landlord, and he said I could sub-let the apartment to you. Still want it?"

"Heck, yes," Ben replied. "I've been looking for a place like yours. What a perfect location near so many software houses. Want me to bring the paperwork and a check over?"

"Well," Nick sighed into the phone. "I'm already out of town. I'm down in Olympia actually on my first stop. Can you scan the paperwork and send me the PDF?"

"Sure," Ben replied.

"Once I get it, I'll call the apartment manager, a Mr. Lam, and tell him you're coming by for the key. I already told him about you."

"Sounds good!" Ben said. "I can't wait."

"Once you're inside, you'll find an envelope on the kitchen counter. It has the wi-fi network id and logon information. And there're a dozen deposit slips for you to pay the rent. Utilities and the rest are on auto-pay and in my name, so everything should run smoothly for you."

"I really appreciate it," Ben said. "Thank you."

"No, thank you. This keeps me from having to dig too deeply into my savings."

"It's great to get away from my old roommates and into my own place. I don't know when those other guys slept. They stay up all night, almost every night, playing and commenting on video games. It's like they didn't get enough screen time at work. I'll have the papers to you in an hour or so; I've got a design review meeting that starts in about ten minutes."

"That's fine. Thanks again, Ben."

"My thanks to you, and don't worry. I'll take good care of the place."

"Appreciate it. Later, man."

"Take care, Nick."

Nick ended the call, let out a big sigh, and walked even taller than his already six-six height back to the hotel.

5

LOCAL FLAVOR

Nick stopped at the front desk on his way to breakfast the next morning. "Oh, hi, Cindy. You were right, my room has a great view to the entire capitol complex."

Cindy smiled up at him. "I'm glad you like it," she responded. "Is there anything you need today?"

"Yes, thanks." Nick pulled on the lanyard that was sticking out of his shirt pocket, bringing a thumb drive out with it. "Is there someplace I can print out a couple files?"

"Of course," Cindy replied. "The Business Center is down that hall and to the right. You probably haven't seen it because you go left to the elevator. It's open twenty-fours a day. Just use your room key to get in. There's no charge for printing."

Nick looked to his left and saw the Business Center sign and the right arrow. "What about a florist? Any nearby?"

Cindy used her left hand to point out the front door. "Just a block and a half down Tenth on the right-hand side."

Nick looked at her left hand and saw that she wore no rings. "Thanks, Cindy."

"My pleasure, Mr. O'Flannigan."

"Nick," he replied.

"My pleasure, Nick," she countered with a slight smile.

Nick put the thumb drive and lanyard back into his pocket, picked up a copy of *The Capital Daily*, and ate breakfast. He got up, cleared his table, and went to the Business Center. The two computers were in Sleep mode as he sat down in front of one, shaking the mouse, then pressing the left key with his right index finger. The screen awoke.

He pulled the thumb drive out of his pocket, stuck it into the one open USB port, and waited for the dialogue box to open. It finally did, and he opened the folder to view the files. Nick had downloaded a map of the local area with highlights of interesting buildings. He'd also found a file that listed some of the state's symbols, such as the state bird, state tree, state flower, state fruit, and some other facts he found interesting. He selected and printed those two files, removed the thumb drive, took the printouts, and went back to his room.

Nick looped the camera bag over his left shoulder, grabbed the small notebook, his phone, and the two sheets he'd just printed. He'd let the maid come in today, so he took the 'Do Not Disturb' sign off the door and hung it on the back side. He pulled the door closed, walked down the stairs, and out the side entrance. He stopped and thought for a moment. He then headed toward Tenth Street. Thanks to two green lights and his long stride, Nick entered Tenth Street Floral in three minutes.

"Good morning, sir," an employee said. "How can I help you?"

"I need a bouquet with a vase that's says, 'Thank you.' I barely know this person, but she helped me, and I want to let her know that I appreciated it."

"Of course, sir," the florist replied. "Do you have a price range in mind?"

"Do you have something in the twenty to thirty-dollar range?" Nick asked.

"Well." The florist's halting voice told Nick he'd have to go a little higher.

"I guess I could go a little higher, but I don't want her to get the wrong idea. They're just to say, 'Thank you'; nothing more." Nick said.

The florist smiled as he opened a display case door, reached in, and pulled out a colorful assortment in a nine-inch vase. "This one is very nice, and it even includes a Rhododendron, our state flower. It's normally forty dollars, but I'll let you have it for thirty-five."

"And a small card to write a note on?" Nick responded.

"They're on the counter. Pick any one you want."

Nick wrote a short note on one of the cards, put it in the envelope, paid for the flowers, and headed back to the hotel.

"Nice flowers," a young woman said as he walked past her. "Lucky lady."

Nick slowed his pace slightly, smiled, but kept on going. He reached Franklin, turned left, and then right into the Capital City Inn lobby. He had the vase in his huge right hand as he approached the desk. "These are for you, Cindy. I love the room. Great views. Thanks."

Cindy's face flushed as she smiled. She tried to say something, but no words came out.

"I'll see you later," Nick said as he turned around and walked back outside.

Nick walked around the area for the rest of the morning, using the map he'd printed. *I didn't think I'd need an entire week just to take some photographs. But there's so much here. I'm glad the schedule isn't any tighter.*

His map showed him the location of several Western Hemlocks, the official state tree. He switched his camera lens to a fisheye one, turned the camera ninety degrees using the optional handle on the Olympus EMIX that he'd purchased just for such occasions, and snapped several photos of the broad-based tree. He turned and started north on Capitol Way when the aromas and the sounds of a food truck assaulted him. He reached the truck and bent his head down to see the chalkboard menu leaning against the side. The pulsating ten-note bass guitar riff of *Louie Louie* was hard to ignore. Nick nodded his head in time with the song's steady beat. *Dut-dut-dut Dut-dut Dut-dut-dut Dut-dut. Dut-dut-dut Dut-dut Dut-dut-dut Dut-dut.*

"Help you, amigo?" the friendly voice came from the truck's open window.

"Yes," Nick said slowly. "Okay. One Beef Chimichanga and a bottle of water."

"Hot, medium, or mild salsa?"

"Mild, please."

"Seven-fifty," the man said as he handed him a bottle of water.

Nick handed the old man a ten-dollar bill. "Keep the change," he said, priding himself on being a good tipper.

"Gracias, amigo." The man's eyes lit up and his broad smile showed a gap in his upper teeth and another one on the opposite side in his lower ones.

"What's with everyone playing *Louie Louie?*"

"The people in Washington have adopted it as the state's rock and roll song. It's not official, but once it got started, it just kept going. Did you know that the song was originally about a Jamaican sailor?"

"I didn't," Nick answered. "I was never able to figure out the words until I looked them up online." Nick saw the reflection in the truck's shiny chrome siding of a couple behind him. He turned around. "I'm sorry," he said. "I didn't hear you come up."

"The music is loud," the man said. "But at least it is as good as the food. This truck is always busy around lunch time."

"So you like it?" Nick said, salivating at the thought of his coming snack.

"No better Mexican in the city."

"Wow. Thanks," Nick said. "I'm glad I found the place then."

"You'll like it; that's for sure. But be careful of his hot salsa. It's a killer."

"Just mild for me," Nick said as the old man handed him a plate covered with aluminum foil. "Thank you," Nick turned back as the couple placed their lunch order. He saw an empty bench, sat down, and ate his Chimichanga.

*They're right; that food is good!* He tossed his trash into a bin, walked around, took more pictures, and then returned to the hotel.

Nick spent the rest of the afternoon sorting through the photos he'd taken so far, organizing them, and putting short, yet informative, labels on each one. He also created a document that named each photo, and he added a short description, such as the one for *Winged Victory*, that was built to commemorate World War I. The bronze statue on the granite pedestal created an impressive visual with the Capitol Building in the background. He uploaded a few to the cloud file that had been created for him, wanting to show Emily, his editor, that he was being both productive and proactive.

After a few hours staring at his screen, he decided to order in and then call it a night.

6

# THE DREADED "BLUE SCREEN"

The incessant buzzing of the alarm clock finally awakened Nick. He showered, shaved, and got dressed. He put a few shirts and other items into the hotel's laundry bag, filled out the slip, and set the bag on the bed. Downstairs, he grabbed the last copy of the paper, ate breakfast, and got a cup of coffee to take back upstairs. *Maybe I should try a local place for breakfast tomorrow.*

Back in his room, Nick set the coffee cup on the desk, sat down, and opened his laptop. He pressed the Power button and heard the machine's whirring as it went through its start-up cycles. Nick popped the lid off the coffee, took a sip, and look at his computer's screen.

It was blank.

The whirring continued.

A blue screen was all that was there.

The whirring continued. And then it stopped.

But the blue screen was still there.

No sound.

No activity.

Just a blue screen.

*I've got to get that checked out right away.* Nick was a bit stressed. Even though his stuff was backed up and on the cloud, he didn't want to buy a new machine this early in the trip.

## 7

## DID SHE DO IT?

Nick closed the lid of his laptop and picked up the phone.

"Front Desk."

"I need a computer repair shop, preferable one that's close by and opens early. I'd look it up myself but my laptop's dead."

"I've got a couple people checking out right now, but if you can come down here in ten minutes, I'll have a few names for you."

"Okay. Thanks," Nick said as he put down the phone, and got things ready to head out.

Nick approached the front desk and recognized the clerk as the one who'd given him the restaurant recommendations. "Great Vietnamese restaurant," Nick said as he licked his lips. "I called down about computer shops."

"Yes," the clerk said as he set a piece of paper on the counter. "This one's on Eleventh, just a block closer than the restaurant, and they're already open."

"Great. thanks," Nick said as he grabbed the slip of paper, scooped up his bags, and speed walked the four blocks to the repair shop.

He pushed the door open and walked up to the empty and shiny counter. He pulled his laptop out of his bag and set it on the counter.

"Hi, there. How can I help you?" the young man behind the counter asked. "Brian" said his name badge.

Nick opened the laptop lid. "I tried to power on this morning and all I got was a blue screen. Everything's backed up to the Cloud, but I need this for my work. The manager at the hotel said you guys are one of the best in the area. Can you look at it right away?"

"Sure," Brian said. "You want to wait?"

"Yes," Nick answered.

The young man closed the laptop, turned it over, and popped out the battery. "Let's check this first." He turned around and took the battery to a large area with numerous battery chargers. He slipped Nick's battery into one and flipped a switch. A green light came on, but just for a short time. The light changed to yellow. Both men watched for a minute. It stayed yellow. Brian turned the charger off and removed Nick's battery.

Brian turned back to Nick. "It still has some charge, so it's not completely dead. But if you're opening a lot of applications and processes during start up, then the battery just doesn't have enough charge to work on its own. It should work okay with a power cord because the battery isn't your laptop's primary energy source. But it won't work on its own."

Nick grimaced. "Do you have one in stock?"

"I'm sure we do," Brian said. "Let me check our inventory and see what we have that is compatible." He went to the computer and typed in the battery's specs. "Yes, we do. Actually, we have two. One's eighty-nine ninety-five and the other's ninety-five. As far I can see, either one should be fine."

"I'll take the one for ninety-five," Nick said.

"Sure," the young man said. "Let me get it and put it in just to make sure you do start up okay."

"Good idea," Nick answered.

Nick's laptop started up promptly with the new battery. "Thanks," he said.

"No problem," Brian said. "And I'd keep this old one as a spare to use with your power cord just in case something happens to this new one."

Nick paid for the battery and walked back to the hotel. "Thanks," he said to the desk clerk who'd given him the repair shop name.

"Everything okay?" the clerk responded.

"It is now," Nick replied as he went to his room.

He set his bag down and called *The Capital Daily*.

"The Capital Daily; how may I direct your call?"

"Local News Editor Mark, please. I'm returning his call." The last part wasn't exactly true.

"Who's calling?"

"My name is Nick, a photographer from Seattle. We spoke a couple days ago."

"Hold please."

"Local news; this is Mark."

"Mark, Nick O'Flannigan calling. We spoke on Monday about the overdose victims at Mercy Hospital. One had the tattoo and one didn't."

"Right, I remember," Mark said.

Nick continued. "I was wondering, actually I was hoping, if you had some time I could come to the paper and talk to you about a couple of things. I won't take up too much of your time."

"We're running up against a deadline, so I don't have

much time," Mark said. "Can you be here in twenty minutes?"

"Sure, I can be there then. Thank you," Nick added as he closed the call.

He didn't grab his camera bag this time. He could always use his phone if he needed to take a picture.

Nick arrived at the newspaper's main office twenty minutes later. He signed in, and was escorted into the newsroom abuzz with conversations, some heated, and people typing away at their computers. "Nice to meet you, Mark. I'm Nick. Thanks for meeting with me," Nick said as the two men shook hands. "I thought a morning paper would be busy mostly at night," he continued.

"That's for the print edition. Our online editions are updated every six hours, so it's pretty much a non-stop effort around here. Not to be rude, but I don't have a lot of spare time," the editor said.

"I understand. I think I told you I'm into macro photography, and I was wondering if you had any other photos or other information about the overdoses that you could share with me. I'm not looking for anything confidential, just items I can look at."

"Why?" Mark asked.

"Because this really intrigues me." Nick paused. "These men were my age. It would really bother me if one my good friends did this."

"And why should I give you access to our photo library?" the editor asked. "You're not a cop or a P.I. are you? Or working on your own story?"

"No, I am on a completely different assignment. I've just found that many photographs hold minute details that most authorities don't see because they're looking for something obvious. It's your story, but I'd like to help any way I can," Nick said. "I didn't know the victims, but I know it had to have affected someone, and affected them deeply."

"That's one thing about working at the paper," Mark began. "You have to tell the story, the facts, just as they are. But deep inside, some of these stories really rip you apart. I do have a few photos that we've not released yet. They came to us from a confidential source, and I'm not at liberty to say who it was or to let you have copies of them."

"I understand," Nick said as the editor clicked on a few icons on his computer screen.

"Here is one from the first victim's room. This is a copy where I've covered the victim's face out of respect for him and his family." Mark clicked on another file. "And here's another one. There's nothing special about them."

"They look like everyday hospital rooms to me," Nick said.

"Exactly. That's partly what's baffling. Why would someone take photographs of everyday hospital rooms?" He then clicked another file and the image popped to the screen. It was similar to the first one he'd shown. "They almost look as if they were taken by a phone or a laptop."

"Wait a minute," Nick blurted. "Go back to the first photo, please."

Mark minimized the image and clicked on the first image.

"See that?" Nick asked. "It's the same nurse in both photos. Who would take pictures of the nurse?"

"I hadn't noticed that before," the news editor said as he went back to the most recent image. "Yes, it is," he added as he zoomed in on her name tag. "Mary Lawson," he read. "Let's go back to the first image, just to make sure."

Mark went back to the first image, zoomed in on the nurse's name tag. "Yep, Mary Lawson," he said. "Hmmm.

Coincidence?" Mark asked as his eyebrows lifted, and his eyes widened.

"You've been in this game much longer than I have," Nick began. "But, two overdoses in the same week at the same hospital, and the same nurse is in the room with them. It seems a bit suspicious to me. Do you want to run a story on it, or call the police?"

"Slow down. I think I'd need a lot more information before I ran a story like that. I'd be putting the paper at risk for a lawsuit if it didn't pan out."

"I know. I'm sorry," Nick replied rather dejectedly." I thought I was on to something."

Mark chuckled. "Don't worry about it. It happens to all of us. You wouldn't believe how many stories I chased just to find they were dead ends or led to other rabbit holes I didn't have time to chase. Hey, but thanks for coming in. It never hurts to have another set of eyes on what we have."

"Sorry I wasted your time," Nick said as he rose from the chair.

"Not a problem," Mark said as he handed him a card. "How long are you in town?"

"Just to the weekend, and then down to Salem."

"Well, don't hesitate to contact me if you discover some real facts, or if you hear anything."

The two men shook hands, and Mark escorted Nick to the lobby.

Nick clicked the hotel address on his GPS device and headed back to the hotel. The flowers he'd given Cindy were on the back counter, but he didn't see her. He took the elevator to the third floor — *I should be taking the stairs* — and went to his room. *Oh, good. Housekeeping has been here.*

Nick flopped down in the somewhat-comfortable chair

in the corner. *Should I, or shouldn't I?* That thought persisted in his brain. Finally, *Yes, I should!*

He looked up the phone number for the Olympia Police Department and called them.

A recording greeted him, telling him if this was an emergency, to dial 9-1-1, and then an option to enter the extension of who you were calling, or dial zero to speak to the receptionist. Nick pressed "0."

"Olympia Police Department, how may I direct your call?"

"Homicide, please," Nick answered.

"Are you reporting a homicide, sir?"

"I'm not sure. I have information about some recent deaths that I think might be homicides."

"Alright. Hold for a moment, please."

"Homicide. Detective Parsons."

"Yes, Detective. I have some information about those recent overdoses at the hospital. I don't think they're overdoses; I think they're homicides."

"May I have your name, sir?"

"My name is," and Nick slowed his speech, "Nick O'Flannigan. That's Capital-O-apostrophe-Capital F-l-a-n-n-i-g-a-n. I'm a professional photographer from Seattle on assignment here in Olympia just for the week."

"Thank you, Mr. O'Flannigan," the detective responded. "And what makes you think those overdoses are homicides?"

"Well," Nick began. "I can't reveal my sources, but I've seen photographs of the hospital rooms where the two men died, and the same nurse was caring for both. Her name is Mary Lawson, and I think she should be looked into."

"Mr. O'Flannigan. We appreciate your interest. But we've already looked into her as we wait for the autopsy results on both men. She certainly had opportunity. But she did not have a motive, and until we see the definitive autopsy results, we don't know that she had means either."

"Maybe no apparent motive," Nick replied. "But think of this. If she was the last one to be with them and gave them meds, then she certainly had access and opportunity. Right?"

"Mr. O'Flannigan," the voice on the line said. "I think you've been watching too many shows on TV. Even if we did suspect her, and we don't," the detective responded. "I can't discuss an ongoing investigation with a journalist."

"Photographer," Nick countered.

"Whatever," the detective said. "I still can't discuss it."

"Was she the one who ordered the prescription for both men?" Nick persisted.

"I'd have to look back at my notes," Parsons answered. "But again..."

"Is she married?"

"I don't know that I'm at liberty to disclose that. What are you thinking?"

"Well," Nick began. "Married or not, what if she wanted revenge, let's say against some young stud who rejected her or maybe even just slighted her? What better opportunity than to pick some guy at random and let him be her victim? Or let them be her victims?"

"Honestly, I thought along the same line. But as I said, I can't really discuss it. That being said, if you do notice something or come across anything you think we missed, feel free to contact us. I do appreciate your call, and I hope you enjoy the rest of your stay here in the capital city."

"Okay. Thanks," Nick said as he disconnected the call. *Wrong again. He really wasn't much of a detective after all. He should just stick to taking photos.*

## 8

# RESTAURANT RECOMMENDATIONS

The slight opening in the drapes allowed some light to enter the room as Nick awoke and turned off the alarm. He showered, shaved, and dressed before opening the blinds completely to his view south and southeast toward the Capitol. He picked up his personalized map and saw where he'd noted a couple restaurants. He looked them up on Yelp and drew a circle around Linda's.

Nick put the "Do Not Disturb" sign on the door, went down the stairs, and headed down Tenth Avenue. He passed the flower shop and saw a line of people standing in front of Linda's for breakfast on the next block. He could smell breakfast as he approached the restaurant. "That good?" Nick asked the person in front of him as he joined the line.

"She's amazing," the old man said. "She only does breakfast six days a week, and then dinners one weekend a month."

"My first time here," Nick responded. "What should I have in case it's my only time?"

"Stuffed French Toast with Homemade Apple Sauce

and a large glass of orange juice. The French Toast is so sweet you won't want to put any syrup on it. And the orange juice is mixed with other citrus for a flavor so distinctive you'll never forget it. You have those two, and I'll bet you'll be back." The man edged forward as the line slowly moved each time someone came out the door.

"Thanks for the recommendation," Nick said. "What about places for dinner?"

"Any place along Columbia Street that's got a view of Capitol Lake. That's if you're into seafood. Otherwise, I'd suggest The Chuckwagon Grille if you want steak or ribs. It's a couple blocks south of the capitol on Water Street. The food's really good and their prices are fairly reasonable. Don't go before five or you'll run into all the old folks like me who are there for the early bird specials."

"Thanks again. Hey, you're almost inside."

The old man chuckled. "Time is one thing I have plenty of."

"Thanks, Linda!" yelled someone who turned his head around as he was leaving the restaurant. Nick's height allowed him to see over the other people in line, and he saw someone in the kitchen waving. *That must be her.*

Nick ordered what the old man recommended, along with a bottomless cup of hot coffee. *I wonder if the paper would be interested in a story about Linda and her following. She's almost like a social media phenomenon without the social media, but in real life.*

"More delicious than I could have imagined," Nick said as the waitress came by.

"Glad you liked it. We're on TripAdvisor if you feel like leaving a review," she said as she handed him the check.

"Will do as soon as I get back to the room."

Nick did as he said he would. He returned to the hotel

room, opened the laptop, and posted a five-star review on TripAdvisor for Linda's, the top-rated restaurant in Olympia. He opened his notebook to see where he would be staying in Salem and a few states beyond. He signed up for the hotel loyalty programs, and then for a couple gasoline programs. *Saving a few bucks on gas will help save my per diem allowance.*

After he posted a few more photographs in the Cloud for the magazine, Nick wrote an email to Emily. *"I'm making good progress,"* the email said. *"And I found out something I'd never heard about Washington. Did you know that 'Louie Louie' is the state's unofficial rock and roll song? How crazy is that?"* Nick completed the email; looked at his Inbox and deleted most of the incoming mail. He went to his bank's site and saw that Ben had deposited the rent. He looked to see what activity was taking place on his macro photography website, and if there was anything for him to moderate or reply to. There was nothing new.

Nick shut down the laptop, grabbed his camera bag, and went back to the capitol campus for some mid-day photographs. He liked it when the sun was pretty much straight up; the shadows came down like holding an umbrella over your head. Nick attached the wide-angle lens to capture the full width of the main campus building, the Legislative Building. It was surrounded by other buildings on three sides plus lots of trees almost all the way around it, and so using the wide-angle lens was the only way Nick could capture the building's full width and height.

He made his way around all four sides of the building and used his telephoto lens to capture some stunning photos of its dome, the tallest self-supporting masonry dome in the U.S. at almost three hundred feet high. The sun was highlighting the Governor's Mansion just a few hundred feet away, and Nick used various filters to get different perspectives the four-story Georgian-style building.

Nick back-tracked to the North Entrance. He waited until the group of school children filed out two-by-two. Several of the youngsters waved to him and said, "Hi" as Nick waved back.

"Do you play basketball?" one of the young girls asked as she craned her head back.

"Not anymore," Nick said. "Do you?'

"No, silly," she replied as she giggled with her friend.

Once they were all out and headed toward the school bus parking area adjacent to the Winged Victory monument, Nick went in. He took a lot of photos in the Rotunda, including the roped-off state seal in the floor. He looked up and went to various locations to get pictures of the five-ton bronze Tiffany chandelier with over two hundred light bulbs. He moved to each corner in the Rotunda for photos of the firepots, similar to ones used to convene the Senate two thousand years ago. He zoomed in on the brass plate on each firepot, "Made by Tiffany & Company, New York."

*I think Emily will like these,* Nick thought as he left the building and returned to the hotel. He downloaded the pictures to his laptop, and also copied them to the thumb drive. He looked out the window and saw the long shadows from the right to the left. Nick retrieved his penciled map and plopped down into the comfortable corner chair. He looked at his map and found the location for the evening's dinner destination.

*I don't care if the old people are there for the early bird specials. The sun's setting, and I'm hungry.*

The old man was right again. The dinner at The Chuckwagon Grille was every bit as good as the breakfast at Linda's. After dinner, Nick returned to his hotel room, and pulled out his main map of the Western States. He saw that it was only about a three-hour drive to Salem, his next capital city. *I wonder if there are any swap meets this weekend where I can look for some old camera gear.* He opened his laptop, and began a search; he found some, but they weren't on the direct route to Salem.

*I've got plenty of time. Besides, I'm going to be on the main freeways for a long time. It'll be okay to have a few side-road trips.*

9

———————————

## THE GOVERNOR

"Governor Returns from Successful Trade Trip" read the headline of Thursday's paper. *The media reception this evening. Shoot.* Nick had forgotten to ask the governor's secretary for an invite. He quickly finished his breakfast, grabbed the paper, and returned to his room.

Nick brushed his teeth, got his camera bag, and headed to the Capitol. His long legs allowed him to maintain a quick pace without actually having to hurry. He entered the North Entrance. It was the same guard he'd seen before on the other side.

"Oh, hi there," the guard said. "Did you ever get to talk with the Governor's secretary?" He opened Nick's bag and did a cursory look inside.

"No," Nick replied. "She was out, and I had some other things to catch up on. But that's where I'm going right now."

"Good luck," the guard said as he handed Nick's bag to him. "The Governor just got back last night, and his office is typically very busy right after he returns." He paused and then offered, "If you'd like, I can call his secretary and tell her you've been here before and you just need two minutes with her. Then it's up to you."

"That's actually all the time I need, if even that. Thanks."

"No problem, man."

Nick went left, following "The Office of the Governor" signs to his left as he heard the guard talking to the secretary. Nick reached the office and saw the well-dressed secretary standing at the open doorway.

"You must be the photographer. The guard did a pretty good job of describing you. I'm sorry, but the Governor is extremely busy today as he just got home from an overseas trip last night. You could wait around and see if he has an opening to take some pictures, but I don't know how long that might be." She finally took a breath.

"Thank you, ma'am. No offense to the Governor, but you are the one I wanted to see. I'm Nick O'Flannigan, and I'm on assignment from *Travel USA* magazine to visit each capital city and take photographs. I saw in Monday's paper that there's a media reception this evening. I know it's last minute," Nick said as he turned on the Boston charm. "I was hoping I could get an invitation to it."

She looked up at Nick. "All the slots have been taken, but I might have an extra card in my desk. Let me take a look," she added as she turned and slowly walked back inside.

Nick crossed his fingers as he waited and watched.

She approached her desk, pulled down on the sides of her sleek dress, and opened the top desk drawer. She reached in fumbled around for a moment. She closed the drawer and walked slowly back outside the main office door. "I couldn't find one. I'm sorry Mr. O'Flannigan."

"Thank you, very much for looking," Nick said.

"You're welcome," the secretary replied. "Sorry I could not help more. Maybe another time?"

"I would if I were in town longer," Nick said as he smiled and gave her hand a slight squeeze. "Thanks again."

"Of course," she echoed as she slowly pulled her hand away. It was sweating. "Sharon," she added.

"Nick," he responded. "Thanks, Sharon." He turned and left the building.

## 10

## THE DISCOVERY

As he walked back to the hotel, Nick's mind wandered back to the alleged overdoses, the nurse, and the things the newspaper editor and the detective had said. Something was bothering him.

"The hospital photographs," Nick blurted out loud as he walked back to the hotel. "I've got to see them again." He picked up his pace, jaywalked across Union Avenue, and entered the hotel lobby. His eyes were focused straight ahead.

"Hi, Nick. Want a fresh cookie?" Cindy held a plate of chocolate chip cookies out and even a little upward toward him.

"Oh. Hi, Cindy. They smell great. Don't mind if I do." A slight smile came across Nick's face as he used a small napkin to select the warm, gooey cookie.

Cindy's eyes opened wider as she stared at Nick's smile.

"Thanks again. Sorry, I'm in a rush. I've got an idea I have to chase down," he said as he turned and went to his room. He set the camera bag on the bed, grabbed the car keys, left the room, and bounded down the back stairs. He pulled into the newspaper's parking lot fifteen minutes later.

*I probably should've called ahead. But then, he might have told me not to come.*

Nick strode confidently into the building and smiled at the receptionist. He spoke slowly. "Hello. I met with the local news editor, Mark, yesterday, and we had some unfinished business. Would you please let him know Nick O'Flannigan is here to see him?"

"Certainly," the receptionist said as she called the newsroom.

"Mark," she spoke quietly into the phone. "There's a tall guy out here to see you. His name is Nick something. Said you two spoke yesterday; something about some unfinished business."

She listened.

"That's what he said."

She listened some more.

"Okay, I'll tell him," she said as she ended the call. She cleared her throat as she looked up at Nick. "I'm sorry, but he's rather busy for the morning deadline. Could you come back this afternoon?"

"Will you do me one more favor?" Nick asked politely. "Would you call him back and tell him I only need two minutes of his time? I swear that's all."

"Well, okay," she replied.

"Thank you," Nick mouthed as she picked up the phone and called Mark again.

"He said just two minutes," she said into the phone as she glanced up at Nick and smiled.

"I'll tell him." She hung up the phone.

"He'll be right out," she said to Nick. She continued in a

soft voice. "He can be rude, though, especially when it's deadline time."

"I won't take long. Thanks again." Nick pulled the Register over and signed in.

The newsroom door swung open wide as Nick rushed through.

Nick smiled and stepped forward with his large hand out to greet him. "Hi, Mark. Thanks. I promise. Just two minutes and then you can throw me out."

"Uh, I don't think that's possible," the News Editor said as his eyes scanned up the tall solid body in front of him. "What do you have now?"

"The photographs," Nick said in a whisper. "There's something about them that's been bugging me. Can we go take a quick look at them again?"

"Okay, but I really am on a tight deadline, and this is the last favor I do for you."

The two men stepped into the frenetic newsroom and went to Mark's desk. He opened the folder on his computer and clicked on the first image.

"No, not that one," Nick said.

Next image. "No."

Next one. "Yes, that one. The one with the pill bottle. Can you go close in on it?"

Mark zoomed in on the bottle; the one with the red and blue capsules spilling out on to the floor.

"Yes. Now can you rotate the image so I can read the label?"

Mark rotated the image; the label was 'upright.'

"Look at that," Nick began. "It's hard to tell for sure, but it looks like it says a quantity of twelve. Is that what it looks like to you?"

Mark lifted his glasses and squinted his eyes. "Yeah. It looks like twelve to me."

"Zoom back out and take it back to the original orientation."

Mark didn't seem like the kind of guy to take orders, but he did what Nick asked. The image was now back to its original position.

Nick began pointing to, and counting, the red and blue capsules. "One, two, three, four, five, six, seven, eight, nine, ten, eleven. There are eleven whole capsules still there."

"I'm not following. How is this new information?"

"Okay," Nick said slowly. "If there were twelve prescribed, and he took only one, he didn't take any more than had been prescribed. It wasn't an overdose, at least not from these pills."

Mark looked up at Nick. "Oh, wow," he said. "Let's find out if the police noticed that too."

He picked up his phone to call the Police Department. Nick stood up straight to stretch out his back from bending over. He looked around the newsroom as Mark spoke softly into the phone.

Mark hung up the phone and looked up at Nick. "They're going to get the remaining capsules from both deaths and send them to the lab for analysis." Mark pushed back his chair, stood up, and shook Nick's hand. "Good work. We might have some new headlines soon."

"Awesome," Nick said as they shook hands. *Maybe there was something to his detective skills after all.*

## 11

## REVENGE

Nick was already awake and dressed when his cell phone rang. He looked at the number, and recognized it as one he'd recently called. "This is Nick."

"Nick, this is Mark from the paper. I know it's early, but I just got a call from the police lab. How soon can you meet me at the paper?"

"It means skipping breakfast, but I can be there in fifteen minutes," Nick replied.

"I'll buy you breakfast. This is huge, and it's because of you."

"I'm on my way," Nick answered. He grabbed his camera bag, slipped his notebook into its side pocket, and pulled his cell phone off the charger. He picked up his keys and headed out of the room and down the stairs to the parking lot. *Slowly. A couple more minutes won't matter.*

He pulled into the mostly vacant parking lot at the paper and went into the empty lobby. He pulled out his cell phone just as Mark came through the door.

"Sorry. I should've told you no one would be here," Mark said as he moved forward to shake Nick's hand.

The two men went through the door into the news-room. It was unusually quiet. Mark pulled up a chair for Nick to sit in. "So," Mark began. "I had a call from the police lab this morning. There was cyanide in all of the remaining capsules from both of the overdose victims. The police are getting a search warrant right now, and are planning to meet us at the hospital in twenty minutes. The nurse is a suspect again, and they're giving us an exclusive on the story, and I want you to go along as my photographer."

"I wasn't expecting this, but I'm ready," Nick replied.

"Okay," Mark responded. "You, my friend," he restarted as he looked directly at Mark, "have probably just solved a murder case. We might not solve it right now, depending on what the cops have a warrant for, but we will solve it."

"Wow," Nick remarked unabashedly. "Who's driving?"

"I will."

The two men arrived at the hospital and saw two police cars already parked there. Mark led the way as they headed to the Administration Building. "Human Resources 312," the sign said. Nick saw four suited detectives standing around as he and Mark exited the elevator on the third floor.

So, what's the plan?" Mark asked.

"We've got a search warrant," one of the officers replied. "It only covers personnel records for now, but we have a judge on standby in case we find anything else and need another one."

"Okay if we follow you in?" Mark replied. "Oh, by the way. This is Nick O'Flannigan who noticed the pill count. He'll be taking photographs for me."

The officers nodded their heads at Nick.

"H.R. is that way," Mark said as he pointed the way

down to 312. The door was open, and the senior officer led the way in.

"Good morning, ma'am," the officer said. "This is a search warrant authorized by a judge to access any and all records pertaining to your employee, Mary Lawson."

"But your people already said she had nothing to do with those deaths," the H.R. rep responded.

"Ma'am. I'm just doing what I'm told to do. You know how the bureaucracy can work sometimes. Believe me, I don't like this any more than you do."

"Let me see the warrant," she replied.

The woman took the warrant and read it. It wasn't the first one she'd read. "Let me give my boss a call," she said after reading it over.

"Of course," the officer said as the H.R. Rep picked up the phone and called the HR Manager.

"Okay," she said into the phone. "Thanks, I'll see you later," she said as she put the phone down. "It'll take me a couple minutes to pull up the records. Want to have a seat?"

"Thanks," the senior officer replied as he looked and saw five empty chairs.

"I'll stand," Nick said as he saw that there was one person more than chairs in the room.

The woman's fingers mis-typed a few letters as she attempted to open Mary Lawson's personnel records. "She's been here a long time. I can print out all the files, but that's a lot of paper."

"To save time and rather than having to pore through her personal papers here," the senior officer interjected, "did Ms. Lawson have any romantic interests or affairs with anyone at the hospital? Or did she ever file any complaints of harassment?"

"Yes," she answered. "It involved Dr. Reynolds, our staff

pharmacist. They had an affair and apparently he promised to divorce his wife to marry Ms. Lawson, but she rejected his overture."

"Who would have the records of which pharmacists prepared the prescriptions that Nurse Lawson had ordered for the two men who died that were labeled as overdoses?" the officer continued with his questions.

"That would actually be in the pharmacy I assume," she answered.

"And who's in the pharmacy right now?"

She looked at her computer screen and clicked on a few icons. Her eyes widened. "Dr. Reynolds."

"You've already been so helpful," the officer soft-toned. "Any chance you would show us where that is?"

She looked at her watch. "I've got about twenty minutes until I really need to be back here."

"Thanks."

The seven—the four police officers, the H.R. Rep, the News Editor, and Nick—left the Administration Building and walked to the main hospital building. They entered the open elevator and the woman pushed the button for the basement. There was little down here other than a hallway leading to a locked door. PHARMACY it said. NO ADMITTANCE was the second sign. A security guard, who had been sitting in a chair next to the door, now stood.

"What's going on?" he said, directing his comments to the hospital official.

"These men have a warrant, and my badge won't open the door, she said. "Will you buzz us in?"

"Can I see the warrant?"

"If you must," Detective Parsons said. "But this matter is urgent."

The guard stared at the officer's badge for a moment, and then slid his keycard into the slot. The door buzzed.

The HR woman went to step inside first, but the detective moved her aside, and the six others walked in.

"What are you doing here?" the stunned pharmacist blurted.

Parsons stepped forward. "Sorry to startle you, Doctor." He looked at his name badge. "Doctor Reynolds. Do you have a few minutes so we could ask you a few questions?"

The doctor looked around. His eyes settled on the security guard.

"And you are?" the pharmacist asked.

"I'm sorry," the lead detective answered. "I'm Detective Parsons," he said as he pulled out his badge and displayed it. "We have just a couple quick questions to ask if you don't mind."

"I'm a little busy," Reynolds replied. "But okay."

"Thank you. Do you know Mary Lawson, a nurse here at the hospital?"

The pharmacist hesitated before answering. "Oh, yes. I've heard of her."

Parsons nodded his head as he looked down at the ring on the pharmacist's left hand. Looking back up, he asked, "Do you know if she's married?"

Reynolds shook his head. "No idea," he answered."

Detective Parsons looked at the mixing table and saw some open red and blue capsules and some powder on top of a small scale.

"Do you ever eat in here?"

The pharmacist's eyes closed slightly as he looked around. "I get breaks, of course. So I don't ever eat in here."

"No," Parson responded. "Never? Right now, I think I smell almonds."

"I have no idea what you're talking about."

"Okay," the detective said as he nodded his head and stepped forward. "Did you ever have an affair with Nurse Lawson?"

The pharmacist looked at the H.R. Rep. "I don't have to answer that, do I?"

She shrugged.

"Let's try that again. Did you have an affair with Nurse Lawson?"

The pharmacist hesitated before answering. "Yes, I did. But we broke it off a while ago. So what?"

"Do you have any cyanide here in the pharmacy?"

"Why would I have cyanide in a hospital pharmacy?" Dr. Reynolds responded.

"I have no idea," the detective said. "I just asked if you do or you don't. It's that simple."

"I don't have to answer that," the pharmacist insisted.

"You don't. You're right. You can wait right here while we search if you want."

His eyes darted toward the scales.

"Do you have something you want to say?"

The pharmacist looked down at his hands and sighed. "She rejected me. I loved her. I would have given up everything for her."

"For who?"

"For her. Mary. I would have left my wife. We could have had a life together. But she—she was mean. Now—now I am ruined."

"So you decided to frame her?"

"If my life is over because of our affair, she should pay too." The pharmacist lunged for the counter, trying to reach the scales and the capsules.

One of the officers grabbed his collar, pulling him back,

but the man was strong, and managed to knock the scale on its side, getting the powder there on his fingers. As another officer tackled him, the pharmacist tried to put his fingers in his own mouth.

The officer stopped him, and between the two, they rolled him over and cuffed his hands. Detective Parsons stepped forward and pulled a little baggie from his pocket. With his other hand, he opened a small pen knife.

He carefully scraped some of the residue from the pharmacist's hands into the little baggie.

"Dr. Reynolds," the detective said formally. "Dr. Reynolds, you are under arrest. You have the right to remain silent. Anything you say can and will be used against you..."

## 12

## TO SALEM

Nick stayed one more day at the hotel. It had rained in the morning. The rising sun shining on the wet dome of the Capitol building provided just the special photos that Nick wanted. He returned to the hotel, organized his photos, uploaded them to the Cloud, and then spent some time photographing the trees in Centennial Park. *Maybe the magazine doesn't want them, but I think they're pretty cool.*

He packed his bag before he headed down to breakfast on Sunday morning. He grabbed a newspaper as he headed into the room where the local TV news was broadcasting the arrest of Mercy Hospital's head pharmacist. The paper's headlines were the same: "Pharmacist Suspected in Recent Overdoses!"

"Dr. Reynold's wife has said that she stands by her husband and that there's no way he would commit any crime," the TV reporter said. Nick looked up at the TV and shook his head. He looked at the paper, and there was his name under the headline. Mark's was first, and Nick O'Flannigan's name was there also. *I wonder if anyone in Seattle reads this paper.*

Nick picked up the newspaper and headed to his room. He got his bags, headed downstairs, checked out, and looked at his new map. He'd found some swap meets selling old camera gear. So instead of heading straight down to Salem, he took I-5 to US-12 to Yakima. Then to Kennewick off of I-82. Then I-84 to Portland, back to I-5 to Salem.

*Maybe a few extra hours, but it's a piece of cake.*

In the meantime, be well. Nick and I will see you as we travel the country together!

# SOME FACTS ABOUT OLYMPIA

Some Facts about Olympia and the State of Washington

- Even though Olympia was named the state's capital city in 1853, it wasn't incorporated as a town until 1859, and a city in 1882.
- Washington became an official U.S. state in 1889, and the rivalry between two other cities (Ellensburg and North Yakima) split citizen votes, enabling Olympia to remain the capital.
- As the largest city and the seat for Thurston County, Olympia is only the 24th largest city in the state and 750th in the U.S.
- The state fruit is the apple; the state vegetable is the Walla Walla sweet onion; the state dance is the square dance; the state insect is the green darner dragonfly.
- Water from artesian wells in Olympia have long been called the reason for great tasting coffee.
- Washington State Patrol is responsible for security and law enforcement on the Capitol

grounds as they are outside the normal jurisdiction of Olympia and Thurston County.

- The Legislative Building, aka the Capitol, has a dome that is 287 feet high, the tallest self-supporting masonry dome in the U.S., and the fifth tallest in the world.
- Some coffee houses in Olympia include Burial Grounds Coffee, Mud Bay Coffee Company, Dancing Goats Espresso Bar, Sizizis, Bar Francis, Maxim, Girls Espresso.
- The nose on the brass bust of George Washington in the Legislative Building has become shiny from visitors rubbing the nose, thinking that will bring them good luck.
- 9.5% of the surface area of the city of Olympia is water.
- Several monuments on the Capitol grounds include those dedicated to World War I, World War II, Korean Conflict, and a POW-MIA memorial.

From the next book, *Slaying in Salem*

Steve needed the money, so he took the second job at the Oregon State Hospital doing security. During the day, he drove an armored truck, a pretty boring job most of the time, although he had fended off a couple of robbery attempts. On that job, he was armed with his weapon of choice, a Ruger Model 97 .45 with nine rounds of "nope, I don't think so" loaded in the magazine.

At the Oregon State Hospital, he carried a baton and a radio, and although he was good with both, it wasn't much reassurance when patrolling the old tunnels under the building. People said areas of the place were still haunted even after the extensive renovations that removed the creepiest parts of the facility, including the old morgue and the room known as the "library of dust" which had contained thousands of copper canisters filled with the cremated remains of residents never claimed by anyone. There was also the story of those once buried in the cemetery. Many of the bodies had been moved, but others had never been recovered.

Not normally a superstitious guy, Steve believed those souls were probably still roaming these halls, waiting to be freed from this world to move on from the next. He had seen and heard things. Light and shadows. Footsteps. He even felt a chill from time to time when he patrolled those tunnels at least once a shift.

Off limits to the public and current residents, the tunnels, now cleaned up, looked like simple hallways with no windows. Water dripped in various places from time to time, but otherwise an empty silence indicated the complete lack of humanity down here. Tonight, the power had unexpectedly gone out in a section down here, so his flashlight was the only light, and he moved it constantly. Do anything down here was the part of the job he hated the most. He felt eyes crawl over him constantly as he walked, the ghost of patients past staring at him from the darkness.

As he rounded a corner, Steve tensed. A former Marine, he could sense something off. Someone was here.

He considered himself to be in good shape, and even at a compact 5'9", there was little that scared him. He flashed his light ahead of himself in the tunnel, and one of the residents stood, staring at what should be a closed wall.

"What's going on, Bill?" he asked. "You okay?"

Bill pointed at himself, and nodded, but didn't speak. He dropped his hands to his sides and looked at his paper slippers. Clad only in the blue scrubs all the residents of the current facility wore, he looked cold.

"You're not supposed to be down here," Steve told him. "What is going on?"

Bill looked up, and there were tears in his eyes. A second later, sobs destroyed his face.

"What is it?" Steve approached slowly and then jerked back as Bill's arm shot up from his side. His finger pointed where the wall should be.

Then Steve felt it. A cold draft that should not be there. Not sure what to be ready for, he raised his baton with his left hand. As he approached Bill at an angle, he could that what must have been a hidden door in the wall was now open, but it was only a rectangle of darkness. "Back up slowly, Bill. You gotta let me by."

The resident did as he was told, his arm still straight out, pointing.

Steve took three deep breaths, trying to slow his racing heart, wishing for a weapon better than a stick. He ducked low, making himself a small target, and poked his head around the edge of the door for a quick glance. As he did, he felt what seemed like cold breath on the back of his neck.

A body, motionless, on an old metal table. Blood dripped from the fingers of its right hand. At first glance, he had not seen anything but the body. He flashed his light around, trying to see if someone remained in the room

.

.

.

All the books in the "Capital City Murders" series are available at www.CapitalCityMurders.com and your favorite e-book seller.

# ABOUT THE AUTHORS

Troy Lambert and Stuart Gustafson are each successful authors in their own rights. As residents of the Great State of Idaho (Troy lives in Meridian, and Stuart is in the capital city of Boise), they have teamed up to bring to you, the reader, this new and exciting series of novelettes **set in each capital city** of the United States of America!

And yes, a total of fifty states means a total of fifty novelettes. Can you handle that? The authors can!

**Troy Lambert** is a full-time writer and author.

Having written over two dozen mysteries and other novels, Troy is well-versed in story creation, and he knows what it takes to make a fictional story real! Troy's hobbies and pastimes (when he's able to break away from the computer) include hiking into the mountains of Southwest Idaho, fishing in a fast-rushing stream, and going for a drive where his mind can work on creating that perfect twist to the book he's currently writing. A native of Idaho Falls, Idaho, Troy and his wife live in Meridian, Idaho.

**Stuart Gustafson** took early retirement in 2007 to spend more time traveling (he's been to 55 countries and 155 cruise ports) and writing (four novels, nine non-fiction books, lots of travel articles). Speaking on cruise ships in many parts of the world has been a great "post-retirement gig," as some have put it. He has leveraged some of the experiences from those travels to insert reality into a few of his mystery novels set in exciting locations around the globe. A native of Southern California, Stuart and his wife live in Boise, Idaho. The majority of his books are available on his website here.